C B 3 3 4 1

This book is presented to:

Given by:

Date:

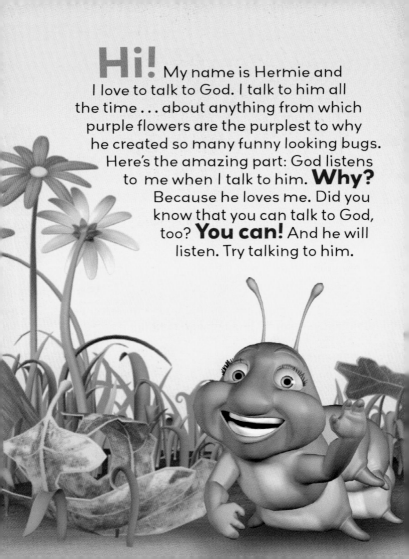

Hi!
My name is Hermie and I love to talk to God. I talk to him all the time … about anything from which purple flowers are the purplest to why he created so many funny looking bugs. Here's the amazing part: God listens to me when I talk to him. **Why?** Because he loves me. Did you know that you can talk to God, too? **You can!** And he will listen. Try talking to him.

Friends

Dear God,

Thank you so much for my friends, especially my family. They really help me to obey your Word. I need people like that in my life. Lord, I know you've told us that we should be friends with other people who love you so that we don't turn away from the truth. Would you please bring the right people into my life so that we can help each other know you better? Thank you, God, because you are my very best friend, and I know you will provide friends on earth for me, too.

AMEN.

Two people are better than one. They get more done by working together. If one person falls, the other can help him up.

ECCLESIASTES 4:9–10

A Broken Heart

Dear God,

I don't feel so well today. What I had hoped would happen didn't, and nothing seemed to go the way I planned. Now I just feel sad and a little angry. Please forgive me for not talking to you about this before now. Sometimes I forget that you are right here beside me. Forgive me, too, for thinking that someone or something would—or should— make me happy. Please help me to remember that you are all I need. Then I know my heart will be happy again. I love you, Lord.

AMEN

Why am I so sad? Why am I so upset? I should put my hope in God. I should keep praising him, my Savior and my God.

PSALM 42:11

Wise Words

Dear God,

When I think about this big world you made, I can hardly believe it. You know so much more than I ever will. But you promised to share your wisdom with me when I needed it, and I need it now.

God, I want to do what is right. I want to do what you want me to do. I pray that you would give me your wisdom. Speak to me through my parents, your Holy Spirit, and your Word. Please help me to obey your will for me. I love you.

AMEN.

If any of you needs wisdom, you should ask God for it. God is generous. He enjoys giving to all people, so God will give you wisdom.

JAMES 1:5

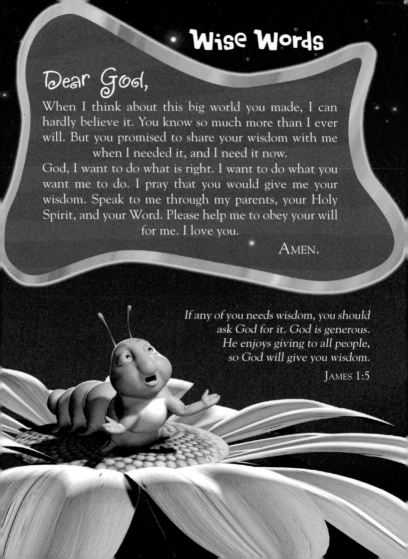

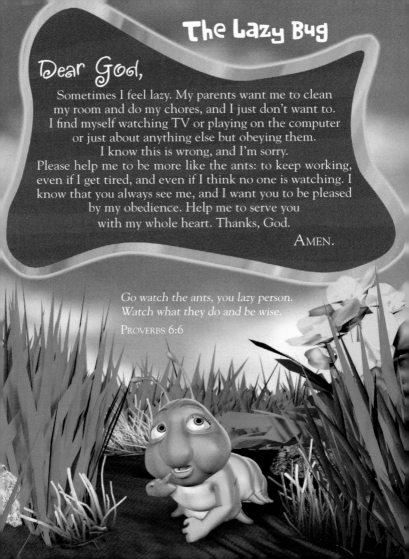

The Lazy Bug

Dear God,

Sometimes I feel lazy. My parents want me to clean my room and do my chores, and I just don't want to. I find myself watching TV or playing on the computer or just about anything else but obeying them. I know this is wrong, and I'm sorry. Please help me to be more like the ants: to keep working, even if I get tired, and even if I think no one is watching. I know that you always see me, and I want you to be pleased by my obedience. Help me to serve you with my whole heart. Thanks, God.

AMEN.

Go watch the ants, you lazy person.
Watch what they do and be wise.

PROVERBS 6:6

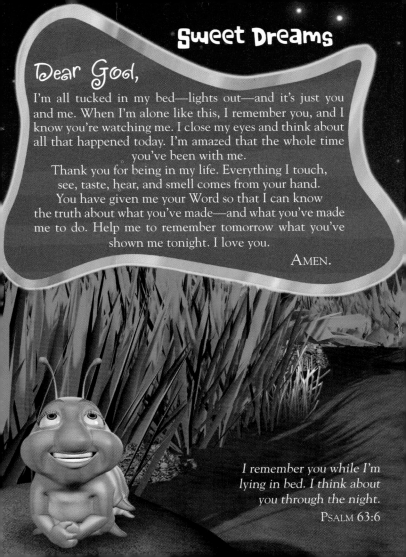

Sweet Dreams

Dear God,

I'm all tucked in my bed—lights out—and it's just you and me. When I'm alone like this, I remember you, and I know you're watching me. I close my eyes and think about all that happened today. I'm amazed that the whole time you've been with me.

Thank you for being in my life. Everything I touch, see, taste, hear, and smell comes from your hand.

You have given me your Word so that I can know the truth about what you've made—and what you've made me to do. Help me to remember tomorrow what you've shown me tonight. I love you.

AMEN.

I remember you while I'm lying in bed. I think about you through the night.

PSALM 63:6

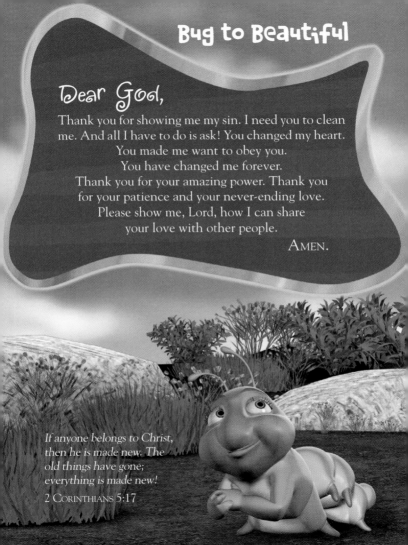

Bug to Beautiful

Dear God,

Thank you for showing me my sin. I need you to clean me. And all I have to do is ask! You changed my heart. You made me want to obey you. You have changed me forever. Thank you for your amazing power. Thank you for your patience and your never-ending love. Please show me, Lord, how I can share your love with other people.

AMEN.

If anyone belongs to Christ, then he is made new. The old things have gone; everything is made new!

2 CORINTHIANS 5:17

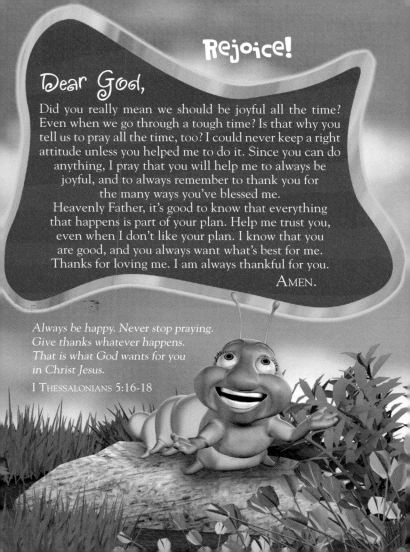

Rejoice!

Dear God,

Did you really mean we should be joyful all the time? Even when we go through a tough time? Is that why you tell us to pray all the time, too? I could never keep a right attitude unless you helped me to do it. Since you can do anything, I pray that you will help me to always be joyful, and to always remember to thank you for the many ways you've blessed me.

Heavenly Father, it's good to know that everything that happens is part of your plan. Help me trust you, even when I don't like your plan. I know that you are good, and you always want what's best for me. Thanks for loving me. I am always thankful for you.

AMEN.

Always be happy. Never stop praying.
Give thanks whatever happens.
That is what God wants for you
in Christ Jesus.

I THESSALONIANS 5:16-18

Dear God,

You already know what's on my mind even before I tell it to you. But sometimes I forget, and I let my problems really bother me. Then I get scared because I know I can't fix them. But you can take what I've messed up and make it right again. So I give you all my worries.

Will you please help me? Help my heart feel calm when I get worried. Thank you for always doing what is right. You are a perfect God. Teach me more about your heart through this hard time. Thanks for your help.

AMEN.

Do not worry about anything. But pray and ask God for everything you need. And when you pray, always give thanks.

PHILIPPIANS 4:6

Do you **ever** wonder what God thinks about **you?** Or what exciting adventures happen to people who believe in him? God has **a lot** to say to us in his Word, the Bible. The Bible is God's special message to us. It tells about what God did and how he wants us to live.

God's Love

Do you have any idea how much God loves you? His love doesn't depend on how you look, how you think, how you act, or how perfect you are. God loves you because he is love, and nothing can change his love for us.

No matter what you do, God has an unstoppable love that you can't be separated from. Ever! "Not death, not life, not angels... nothing now, nothing in the future, no powers, nothing... in the whole world will ever be able to separate us from the love of God" (Romans 8:38–39). Isn't that so cool!?!

So run to Jesus. He wants you to love him so much that there's no room in your heart and life for sin. Invite him to come and live in your heart. Let him fill your heart with his love.

Truth

Jesus said, "If you continue to obey my teaching, you are truly my followers. Then you will know the truth. And the truth will make you free" (John 8:31–32).

Sometimes it's hard to tell the truth, huh? Especially if you know you are going to get in trouble for something ... like if you hit your brother or sister and your parents ask you if you did it, it may seem easier to just lie so you won't get in trouble.

Or maybe you exaggerate a story to impress your friends. We may call it stretching the truth, but God calls it a lie.

Jesus wants you to be a truth teller ... all the time. Telling the truth makes you free. If you aren't always honest, start today. Be just like Jesus. Tell the truth, the whole truth, and nothing but the truth.

THE FAMILY RESOURCES CENTER
321 MAIN STREET
PEORIA, ILLINOIS 61602
(309) 637-1713

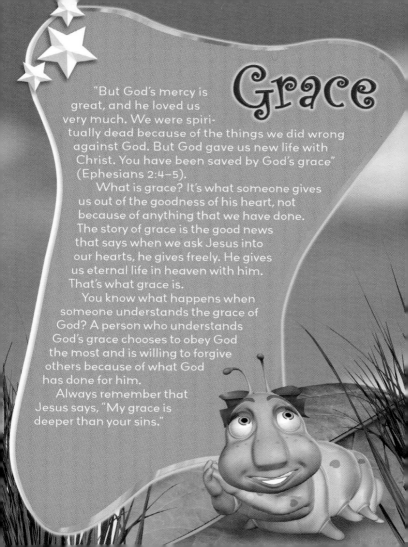

Grace

"But God's mercy is great, and he loved us very much. We were spiritually dead because of the things we did wrong against God. But God gave us new life with Christ. You have been saved by God's grace" (Ephesians 2:4–5).

What is grace? It's what someone gives us out of the goodness of his heart, not because of anything that we have done. The story of grace is the good news that says when we ask Jesus into our hearts, he gives freely. He gives us eternal life in heaven with him. That's what grace is.

You know what happens when someone understands the grace of God? A person who understands God's grace chooses to obey God the most and is willing to forgive others because of what God has done for him.

Always remember that Jesus says, "My grace is deeper than your sins."

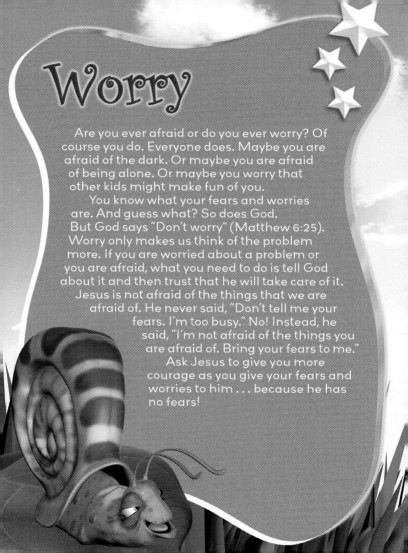

Worry

Are you ever afraid or do you ever worry? Of course you do. Everyone does. Maybe you are afraid of the dark. Or maybe you are afraid of being alone. Or maybe you worry that other kids might make fun of you.

You know what your fears and worries are. And guess what? So does God. But God says "Don't worry" (Matthew 6:25). Worry only makes us think of the problem more. If you are worried about a problem or you are afraid, what you need to do is tell God about it and then trust that he will take care of it. Jesus is not afraid of the things that we are afraid of. He never said, "Don't tell me your fears. I'm too busy." No! Instead, he said, "I'm not afraid of the things you are afraid of. Bring your fears to me." Ask Jesus to give you more courage as you give your fears and worries to him . . . because he has no fears!

Decisions

Have your friends ever asked you to do something that you knew wasn't right? You may have felt pressured into making a decision at that very moment. These types of decisions will happen your whole life, so you must prepare yourself to make the right choices by fixing the truth of God's Word, the Bible, firmly in your heart.

When you face tough decisions, you have to know what is right and wrong, and God's Word can help you do that. You will still need to pray for courage, but doing right begins by knowing the truth in your heart and mind.

Don't ever make a decision based on what other people are doing or what is popular. You must listen to God. God says you're on your way to becoming a follower of Jesus when you can decide between what is right and wrong. So, do what is right.

Be honest. Take a stand. Be true! You won't ever regret it.

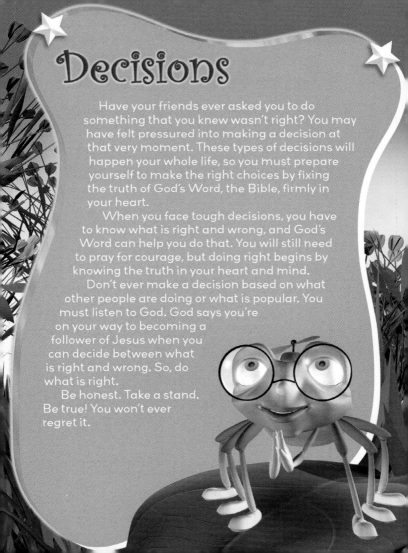

Suffering

Do you ever think that life is just unfair? Maybe your team loses a game or you get sick on the day your class was supposed to take a fun field trip. The truth about life is that sometimes bad things happen ... even to good people.

But did you know that in heaven there is no pain or suffering? That's right! Jesus died for you so that you can have a home in heaven without any sadness or pain.

But while you are living here on earth, God will help you through tough times. God is always with you. Always! He says that he will never leave us ... especially in hard times.

The apostle Paul said, "We have small troubles for a while now, but they are helping us gain an eternal glory. That glory is much greater than the troubles" (2 Corinthians 4:17). When we see Jesus in heaven, any suffering we went through on earth will be worth it. Ask God to help you understand. And when you cannot understand, just trust him.

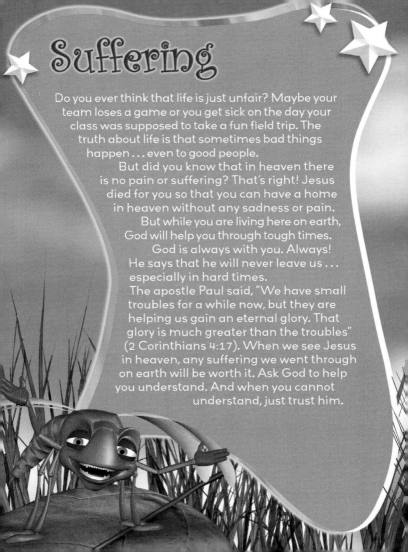

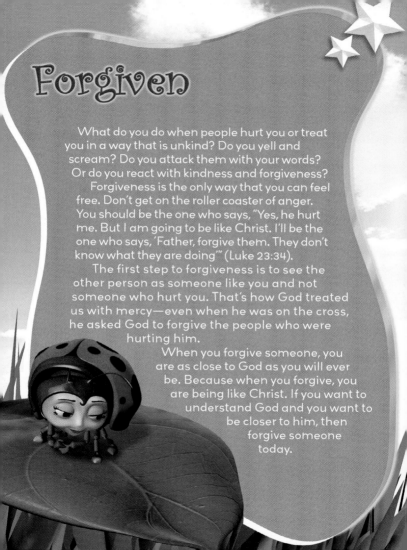

Forgiven

What do you do when people hurt you or treat you in a way that is unkind? Do you yell and scream? Do you attack them with your words? Or do you react with kindness and forgiveness?

Forgiveness is the only way that you can feel free. Don't get on the roller coaster of anger. You should be the one who says, "Yes, he hurt me. But I am going to be like Christ. I'll be the one who says, 'Father, forgive them. They don't know what they are doing'" (Luke 23:34).

The first step to forgiveness is to see the other person as someone like you and not someone who hurt you. That's how God treated us with mercy—even when he was on the cross, he asked God to forgive the people who were hurting him.

When you forgive someone, you are as close to God as you will ever be. Because when you forgive, you are being like Christ. If you want to understand God and you want to be closer to him, then forgive someone today.

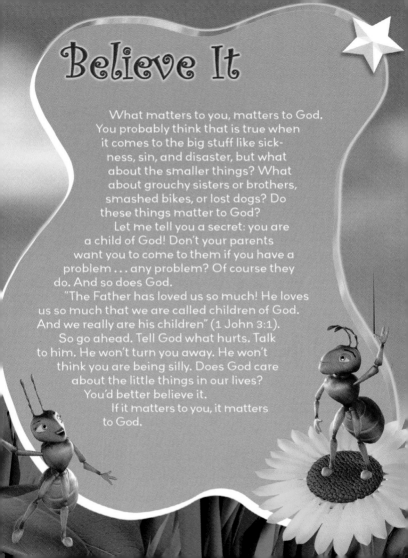

Believe It

What matters to you, matters to God. You probably think that is true when it comes to the big stuff like sickness, sin, and disaster, but what about the smaller things? What about grouchy sisters or brothers, smashed bikes, or lost dogs? Do these things matter to God?

Let me tell you a secret: you are a child of God! Don't your parents want you to come to them if you have a problem . . . any problem? Of course they do. And so does God.

"The Father has loved us so much! He loves us so much that we are called children of God. And we really are his children" (1 John 3:1). So go ahead. Tell God what hurts. Talk to him. He won't turn you away. He won't think you are being silly. Does God care about the little things in our lives? You'd better believe it.

If it matters to you, it matters to God.

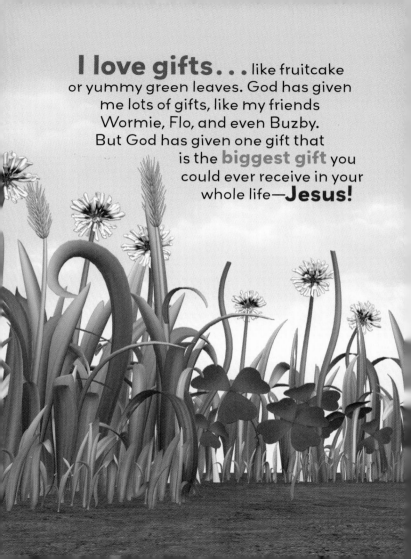

I love gifts... like fruitcake or yummy green leaves. God has given me lots of gifts, like my friends Wormie, Flo, and even Buzby. But God has given one gift that is the **biggest gift** you could ever receive in your whole life—**Jesus!**

God sent his only son Jesus to earth
from heaven to save us. **Why?**
Because we make bad choices
and do things that are wrong.
These wrong choices are called sins.
But Jesus saves us from our sins.
How? He died on a cross for us.
And because he did, we can someday
live in heaven with him forever.

What an amazing gift!

*But God gives us
a free gift—life forever
in Christ Jesus our Lord.*
ROMANS 6:23

What does God want you to do?
Have you ever thought of a gift
you can give to God? What do you think
God would like more than anything
else in the world? He wants you
to believe in him and love him, too.

How can you do this?

You can follow
three simple steps:

1. Believe in Jesus. Know that Jesus is God's Son who came to earth to teach you how to live, to die to take away your sins, and to give you life forever in heaven.

"If you use your mouth to say, 'Jesus is Lord,' and if you believe in your heart that God raised Jesus from death, then you will be saved."
ROMANS 10:9

2. Ask God to forgive you for the things you do that are wrong. When you do something that you know is wrong, it is called sin. Jesus died to take away our sins.

"But if we confess our sins, he will forgive our sins. We can trust God. He does what is right. He will make us clean from all the wrongs we have done."
1 JOHN 1:9

3. Follow him. The rest of your life will be a great adventure as you learn how Jesus wants you to live and follow him!

Jesus talked to the people again. He said, "I am the light of the world. The person who follows me will never live in darkness. He will have the light that gives life."
JOHN 8:12

Deciding to follow Jesus is the most important decision you will ever make. You can start **now** by praying this prayer:

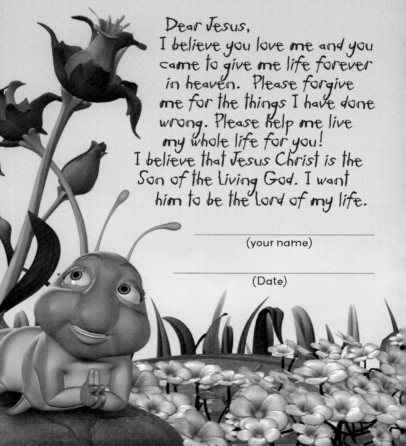

Dear Jesus,
I believe you love me and you came to give me life forever in heaven. Please forgive me for the things I have done wrong. Please help me live my whole life for you!
I believe that Jesus Christ is the Son of the Living God. I want him to be the Lord of my life.

_____
(your name)

_____
(Date)

Now that you've placed your trust in Christ, you can take three steps. Just think of these three words. They each start with a "b": **b**aptism, **B**ible, and **b**elong.

Baptism shows and celebrates our decision to follow Jesus. *Jesus said, "Anyone who believes and is baptized will be saved"* (MARK 16:16).

Bible reading brings us closer to God. God has a lot to say to us through his Word, the Bible. We learn more about him by reading the Bible. *"I have taken your words to heart so I would not sin against you"* (PSALM 119:11).

Belong to a church. As part of God's family, it is important for you to attend church. Get involved. Make friends. Worship God together. A Christian without a church is like a baseball player without a team. You need the church to make you stronger. *"You should not stay away from the church meetings, as some are doing. But you should meet together and encourage each other"* (HEBREWS 10:25).

These three steps—**baptism**, **Bible** reading, and **belonging** to a church—are important steps to your faith.

May God bless you
as you follow him!

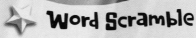

Word Scramble

See if you can unscramble
these New Testament words:

ECRGA

_____

ELVO

_____

PSICELID

_____

YCAALVR

_____

LGNEA

_____

SWEI NME

_____

RSVAOI

_____

(grace)
(love)
(disciple)
(calvary)
(angel)
(wise men)
(Savior)

In Other Words . . .

How many words can you make from these words?

Salvation: _____
_____
_____
_____

Forgiven: _____
_____
_____

Jerusalem: _____
_____
_____

Christian: _____
_____
_____

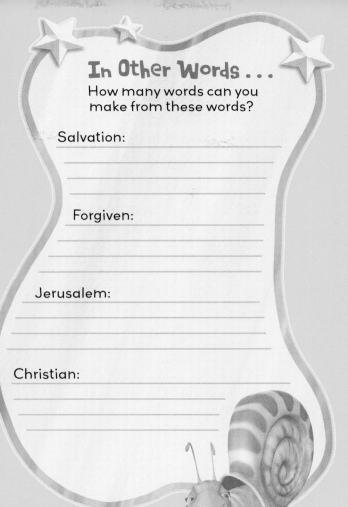

Find as many words as you can that describe love:

```
T P A T I E N T R E
H K L R P R E S K I
O H I U O U H S I N
U G I S F T I S N M
G I F T L O F E D E
H H O P E V T R W T
T U H F O R E V E R
F M A T I L O N T U
U B S E R V A N T T
L L G T J E S U S H
O E S H A P P Y E U
```

patient, kind, thoughtful, trust, humble, gift,
servant, forever, Jesus, happy, truth, hope

Favorite Things

God has made the world and all that is in it. Lots of things make me happy. Here are some of my favorite things:

Favorite color: _____

Favorite season: _____

Favorite kind of pet: _____

Favorite drink: _____

Favorite room of the house: _____

Favorite game: _____

Favorite book or story: _____

Favorite TV show: _____

Favorite songs: _____

_____

_____

Favorite Bible verses:

_____

_____

_____

Favorite holidays:

_____

_____

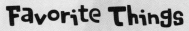

Some of my favorite Bible animals are:

_____ _____

_____ _____

_____ _____

Draw a picture of one of your favorite animals next to Hermie. Maybe they could be friends!

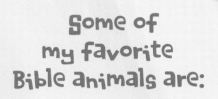

Some of my favorite Bible stories are:

If I could travel in time to visit one of these stories, I would choose _____

_____.

I would like to go there because I would like to see what was going on or be a part of the action. Here's what I'd like to see or do most from that story: _____

_____

_____

_____

_____

_____

_____

_____

_____

Some of my favorite Bible characters or people are:

_____ _____

_____ _____

_____ _____

If I could be any one of
these people, I would be

_____

Here's why I'd like to be that person:

_____

_____

_____

_____

_____

_____

_____

THE FAMILY RESOURCES CENTER

Family Resources Center
415 NE Monroe,
Peoria, IL 61603 (309) 839-2287